WILD
COUNTRY

To Amy and Mark Kasin,

Welcome to wild country!

David Harris

2/2/01

WILD COUNTRY

Outdoor Poems for Young People

BY DAVID L. HARRISON

Wordsong/Boyds Mills Press

To Jennifer and Jeff
Love, Dad

—D. L. H.

Text copyright © 1999 by David L. Harrison

Published by Wordsong
Boyds Mills Press, Inc.
A Highlights Company
815 Church Street
Honesdale, Pennsylvania 18431
Printed in China

Publisher Cataloging-in-Publication Data

Harrison, David L.
   Wild country / by David L. Harrison.—1st ed.
   [48]p. : ill. ;   cm.
Summary: A collection of poems celebrating nature
ISBN 1-56397-784-2
1. Nature-Juvenile poetry. 2. Children's poetry, American.
[1. Nature-Poetry. 2. American poetry.]   I. Title.
811/ .54   dc21   1999   AC   CIP
Library of Congress Catalog Card Number 98-88337

First edition, 1999
The text of this book is set in 14-point Clearface Regular.

10 9 8 7 6 5 4 3 2

CONTENTS

MOUNTAINS

Giants 6
Love Song 7
Mountain Flower 8
Eaglet 9
Summer Vacation 10
Vapor Trails 11
Glacier 12
Dall Sheep 13
The Mountain 14
Storm 15

HIGH COUNTRY

High Country 16
Valley of the Elk 17
River Run 18
Wolf 19
Walking in Tall Grass 20
Raven 21
Mama Bear 22
Above the Tree Line 23
Musk-Oxen 24
Star Watch 25

FOREST

Enchanted Forest 26
Crossing Paths 27
The Glimpse 28
Bear Country 29
Landlords 29
The Pond 30
Last Days of Fall 31
Butterflies 32
Song of the Tree Frogs 33
Moose at Dusk 34
Salmon 35
Spring Bug 36
Caribou 37

SEA

Breaking Through 38
Beyond Measure 39
Low Tide 40
Seagulls 40
Sandpipers 41
Eyes of the Forest 41
Bachelor Sea Lions 42
Puffin 43
Seal 44
Starfish 44
Sea Otter 45
Thief! 46
Humpback 47
No Words 48

MOUNTAINS

GIANTS

All nose and toes and knobby knees
the giant mountains sprawl.
In tangled piles and crooked files
they loiter over all.

LOVE SONG

Hear that?

Like a rifle shot
somewhere high
among the ledges?

Or a rock
falling on a rock?

Bighorn rams
are banging heads,
choosing winners.

This time of year
mountains have few secrets
and rams make noisy neighbors
when they want wives.

Mountain Flower

Blue flower
clinging for life
to this rocky slope

Fragile blossom
hiding from wind
that chills the night

Tiny oasis
in a barren world
how do thirsty insects find you
crouching among the gray rocks?

EAGLET

Not quite ready,
he sits on the family nest
and calls for food.

Soon he must leave.
Soon he'll be ready,
but today the world
still looks too big,
the future uncertain.

Not quite ready,
he sits on the family nest
and waits for food.

SUMMER VACATION

Snowless in August,
the mountain lies
quiet, shaded, cool.

Later the valley
will echo with skiers
with breath streaming
like white scarves.

For now
the mountain counts
forget-me-nots,
listens to squirrels,
and rests.

VAPOR TRAILS

Vapor trails crisscross the blue
chalkboard sky in
rail-straight lines

Gradually lose their taut fitness
their laser focus
their dedication

Dwindle to wandering wisps
that fade away
like tissue
on a pond.

Vapor trails set out importantly
but soon
they're
gone.

GLACIER

River of blue-cold ice
frozen in slow motion
flowing an inch a day

You polish mountains
scoop out basins
sculpt valleys

An inch a day
an inch a day
and you're not done.

DALL SHEEP

White speck on the peak,
what can you see
from your point of view
just a nimble leap
below the sky?

We're stuck down here
on the valley floor
like ants.

What's coming?
Can you see?

The Mountain

"Approach if you dare,"
you say, knowing full well
how much we yearn
to stand on your highest peak
and gaze down on the world,
to dare!

"Climb my bony shoulders,"
you say, winking through clouds
you wear like a hat
on your cold white head.

"I'll clasp you to my breast
and when I let you go—
if I let you go—
you can tell your friends back home
you dared!"

Storm

Clouds on the mountain
are somersaulting today.

Thundering back
at the shrieking wind
they flash like fire
among the peaks,

But in spite of complaints
the clouds on the mountain
are head-over-heeling
somersaulting today.

HIGH COUNTRY

HIGH COUNTRY

High country sings its own wind-song
of flowers dressed for spring's brief fling,
snow-water breaking on ledges.

Wind-song sings
of eagles winging canyon walls,
salmon leaping falls,
caribou bands spread under stars,
solitary moose in marshes.

High country sings its own wind-song
of nights that chill and days that burn.
"Leave if you must," it sings, "but you'll return."

VALLEY OF THE ELK

The valley is wide and long,
bowed gently like a tongue,
its sides guarded by sudden woods.

At a half mile
they're a big dot and a little dot,
tan against pale green.

We fumble for binoculars too late.
In big bounds and little bounds
they leap for the trees.

Another lesson,
another day wiser
in the valley of the elk.

River Run

Like cold thread you fly
through the eye of the canyon
pulling our boat over rocks
wet for a thousand years.

We hit a knot and scream
(bravely) in your frigid spray
then spin around a turn
and rush away.

High on the wall a Dall sheep
goes on grazing.

WOLF

One wolf
in a field
in full light—

One wolf
in full view
like a big dog,
shaggy, gray,
but

it's a wolf,
casual
about being a wolf,

moving one foot at a time
through tall grass,
hunting.

WALKING IN TALL GRASS

Small toad
half an inch tall
in grass that strikes me
waist high

Small toad
with fragile bones
living in a harsh world

Small toad
looking for bugs
knows nothing of me

I must watch for us both

Raven

At the top of the dead tree
with the dying sun at your back
you perch like a totem
carved from black wood
and croak out your soul song.

Alone in the world
you mutter to yourself
sounds of old sadness
and ancient truth.

Raven, you surprise me
with your size
and your beautiful feathers
and your ugly old
sad song.

MAMA BEAR

Down the valley
where the willows grow
and paintbrush paints
the meadow yellow,
you bring your cubs to breakfast.

The berries are ripe!
Take your time.
Red strawberries
reward the tongue
with sticky sweet jelly.

It's a fine sunny day
to stroll with your cubs,
the sort of day
to lick your lips.
Have another berry.

ABOVE THE TREE LINE

High above slopes
where no tree grows
air bites
and life belongs
to the strong.

Plants crouch
on stingy soil
and survival counts
on fur and shaggy wool.

High above slopes
where no tree grows
cold wind blows
and life belongs
to the strong.

MUSK-OXEN

Shaggy beasts
with the wind in your wool,
you graze the tundra unafraid,
unchanged since who knows when.

When wolves come
sniffing your babies,
they find you shoulder to shoulder,
long faces like death masks,
horns like swords
curved at your sides,
granite skullcaps lowered
to slam wolves and break bones.

You look disagreeable,
formidable,
dangerous.

Who wants to taste your babies
that much?

Star Watch

Cocoon-like I drowse
by pinewood sparks,
gazing at stars.

How many there are,
how far,
how clear their light
on this frosty night.

My eyelids droop.
I'm at home in the dark,
sleeping in the company of stars.

FOREST

ENCHANTED FOREST

Sunlight looks green,
slanting through limbs
wrapped like mummies
in green moss-rags.

No sound, no sound
but the raven calling
. . . somewhere.

Small squirrel
walks up a tree,
pauses on the first limb,
takes a good look,
listens . . .

The forest is listening,
breathing,
watching.

Is it talking?
I don't know the words.

CROSSING PATHS

A single hoof mark
in the moist trail

Small
probably a deer

We'll never meet
yet our paths cross
here

In these woods
our separate ways
are clear

But standing briefly
where this deer stood

Is a memory
worth taking
beyond the woods

THE GLIMPSE

Where treetop winds
rattle limbs like dry bones
and snowmelt waterfalls
sing stony songs
something moves

Something glides
between wide trunks
where sunlight smudges
trick the eyes

Something cautious
soundless
pauses . . .

What?

. . . sniffs
      is gone.

BEAR COUNTRY

There's a bear nearby.
Can you feel him?

Somewhere close
he sniffs the air,
hears us, smells us,
knows we're here.

He's deciding
if he cares.

There's a bear nearby.
Can you feel him?

LANDLORDS

Flies own the shady places,
all the best places
where you want to rest,
soak your feet,
eat a peach.

Slyly they size you up
for tenderness,
set their price
for using their shade

Then they send you packing,
slapping, swatting,
seeking safety
in the cheap, sweltering sun.

THE POND

Deep in the woods,
where still trees
drip green moss
and mushrooms litter
the spongy earth
like fairy tents,
lies a round pond.

A long age ago
some glacier dug
and scooped this place
for a perfect pond
where wary creatures
pause to drink
and light-footed birds
walk on lily-pad
stepping stones.

What if the glacier
had not dug here?
Where would
the animals drink?

Last Days of Fall

Like helicopters
dragonflies buzz the pond

In spite of drizzling rain
their hunt goes on

Days of easy meals
will soon be gone

BUTTERFLIES

Palettes of pigment
daubed on blossoms,
streaked on tree limbs,
stippled on meadows,
splashes of color
dashed off quickly.
Masterpiece.

Song of the Tree Frogs

At the edge of night
the sun pulls down
its soothing shade
and peepers creeping
from leafy covers
tune up to sing.

Who will start
this evening's song
with fluted notes
that serenade the night?

Someone begins,
the same song
his ancestors sang,
and the forest fills
with an urgent chorus.

It must be high honor,
if you're a frog,
to sing the evening's solo
so others will get it right.

Moose at Dusk

At shadowy dusk,
when trees take faces
and stones move,
I hurry for home
thinking only
of leaving the forest
before full dark—
I've stayed too long.

When from the deepening gloom
you materialize
like a phantom beast —
high shouldered, massive,
mute.

Caught by surprise
(uncomfortable)
I stare,
thinking how easily
you knew I was here.

Before my eyes you blend
with shadows, disappear.
I cannot blink you back,
but still you're there.

Knowing I'm not alone,
I double my steps
and jog for home.

Salmon

The final journey begins
without apparent reason,
browsing through blue salt water
to a certain burbling stream
where mouthfuls of familiar current
bring messages from home.

Something stirs deep needs,
urgently pumps out signals
to lunge through frantic waters,
leap up the crooked
roaring path to home.

Exhaustion ends the struggle,
sends the final code—
to mate and then to drift—
assuring that other journeys
will begin.

SPRING BUG

Maybe the bug was young
or running from something
or careless.

Anyway it fell
from the willow leaf
into the water
floated on the surface
a couple of seconds
then swam for the bank
as fast as it could.

Made it almost.

Then something below
exploded up under
all mouth and popping eyes
and the bug was gone.

Water closed over
like nothing had happened
and babbled on.

CARIBOU

He walks kingly
through willow thickets,
antlered crown high,
while we, like subjects,
watch him pass,
and sigh.

BREAKING THROUGH

Down the mountains
down the high country
to the forest and beyond
to the far side of the forest
you break through to the sea

And suddenly there is nothing else
and nothing else you need.

BEYOND MEASURE

Three things the eye
cannot perceive:
the number of stars,
the height of the sky,
the depth of the sea.

Low Tide

At low tide
the wet sand lies cluttered
like a table
after dinner guests leave
with wadded seaweed napkins
flung among sand-dollar cookie crumbs
and shell coins
left as tips for good service.

Seagulls

Mewing like cats
they fly all day
this way and that
crying
for lost balls of yarn.

SANDPIPERS

Light-footed sandpipers
trip down the beach
darting for tidbits
dodging the tide
like tourists wearing
their Sunday shoes.

EYES OF THE FOREST

Boats throb by
the endless shore
as people gasp at whales
and point to porpoises.

They do not see
the proud heads,
white dots
on green boughs.

The silent forest
watches with
its eagle eyes.

Bachelor Sea Lions

Bachelor sea lions
sit on the rocks
bellowing out their sorrow.

Next year,
maybe,
they'll win the fight.

Next year,
maybe,
they'll win a mate.

Not this year.
Not this year.

Bachelor sea lions
flop on the rocks
bellowing out their sorrow.

PUFFIN

You pop from your burrow
dressed for the game—
black uniform,
white and black helmet,
orange noseguard,
yellow plume.

"Go out for a long one!"
your stomach yells.

You leap in the air,
a forward pass,
your football body
pumps and slants
through interfering
cormorants

To splash headfirst
in fishy water.

Touchdown!

SEAL

Little seal,
furry little iceberg
bobbing in the bay,
take my advice—
keep your distance,
slip away!

STARFISH

Muscle-bound with arms that pry,
starfish dine on fresh oysters
and leave their shells to litter beaches
like dirty dishes.

Sea Otter

Rain is weeping
from a sky
the color of the sea
and I
feel cold and gray,

But when we pass you
bobbing there,
catching forty winks
in bed,

I lift my head
to watch you yawn
and chuckle
at your nonchalance.

THIEF!

Jaeger, you pirate-bird,
the gull doesn't see you
moving so swiftly,
sneaking behind.

Jaeger, you bully-bird,
stealing a meal
from that hungry gull.

Jaeger, you thief-bird,
soar away satisfied,
your day's work done.

HUMPBACK

"There!" someone yells.
We rush to look.
"See his spout?"

We breathe like we're praying.

Your great humped back
breaks the sea,
rolls, disappears
like the gray rim
of the last setting sun.

Silent, uncertain,
we float on the sky
of your world.

Are you gone?
Will you come back?

Can you?

No Words

No words
are as big as a mountain,
blue as a summer sky,
flickering quick
as a hummingbird's wing,
bright as a butterfly.

No words
taste as sweet as wild honey,
glow like a setting sun,
howl at the moon
like wolves in the night,
leap like a stag on the run.

No words
can paint pictures of nature,
they're poor shabby symbols at best
that only remind us
that beauty surrounds us,
the heart must supply the rest.